THIS BOOK BELONGS TO

____

For more information contact:
Independent Authors Publications
PO Box 7062,
Roselle, NJ 07203
www.independentauthorspublications.com

Cover Design – Webprint Lab
Edited – Catherine Felegi

Print ISBN: 978-1-950974-05-4
Digital ISBN: 978-1-950974-04-7

DEDICATION

To Grando, the angelic being who raised me,
and to Cherrand my big sister
with whom I began this journey.

Frolicking Frogs

Written by Marie Laurencin

Illustrated by Muriel Numao

Miss Conduct made sure that the report to the headmaster was swift and included full details, which even prompted the headmaster to put his hand over his mouth in shock and dismay

- a man who was not given to hyperbole.

Miss Conduct woed and moaned about when she took the six
frogs to the marshes for a long weekend.

They behaved so badly - they placed their wellies on their hands
and their gloves on their feet,
causing infectious laughter to spread throughout the bus.

This made it difficult, she said, for her to keep the rest of the class calm during the bus ride. The others began to sing loudly, "Here we go! Here we go! Here we gooooooo!" Miss Conduct tried her best to keep the students calm, but things fell apart completely when Miss Take's wig slipped aside during one of her many attempts to manage the sways from the bus ride. Miss Take, the assistant teacher, came to the rescue by asking the students to play a guessing game. She asked the class to guess the name of the next village on their journey. The prize was an unmissable new mobile phone ringtone, which she promised none of them had heard before.

When the bus stopped for refreshments, it was raining, so the six went out carrying their umbrellas upside-down, catching the rainwater to drink. They poured it on each other, soaking one another in an unholy mess that required each to change their clothes.

Next, they stuck their tongues out so far when licking their ice-creams, they frightened the residents of Dragonfly Village. Some of them allowed their ice-creams to melt and stream down between their fingers, licking hard, making a disgusting sucking sound in between licks - luuuuup, suuuuurp suuurp luuuup! Luuuup, suuuuurp suuurp luuuup. This, she found particularly hard to bear.

DRAGONFLY VILLAGE

"At one point," Miss Conduct carried on, "the six even sang at the top of their voices. 'CAAAAR-OAK, CAR-ORK, CAR-ORK, CAR-OAK, CAAAAR-OAK,' swinging altogether from one swing-seat at the park in the marshes. This frightened the other marsh users and embarrassed the rest of the class! And so, Headmaster Ben, I am requesting to not take these six to the savannah next week, nor to the marshes, and even more so, not to Port-of-Spain."

The following day, she informed the six and their parents that they would not be allowed on the next school trip.
But the six had other ideas.

They found out the details for the next school trip from their friend, and decided that they would make their own way there!
Going to Port-of-Spain should have been easy, except the six had gotten on a bus heading to San Fernando, which was 20 kilometers in the opposite direction.
First, they pulled mini-crackers in the back of the bus. The smell of the stale smoke made the old ladies at the front of the bus dizzy and nauseous. The six giggled hard at jokes told incomprehensibly through tear-streaked laughter. Then they began to tell rude jokes openly. Their laughter grew so loud that the other passengers threatened to report them. They kept their cellphones on loudspeaker for most of the journey, exchanging videos and music, from calypsonians and rappers.

They showed little mercy towards the other
passengers, until a Billy goat got up and
bleated, "Quiiiii- quiiiii- quiet!" The Billy goat's horns looked so fierce
that they
resorted to riddles and rhymes for
made-up prizes.

Suddenly, the bus came to a screeching halt. The six were to be thrown
off the bus! The other passengers had had enough when they
started shooting one another with water
pistols. The bus driver would radio for
assistance if the six did not hop off, so the six left rather sheepishly.

Now, they had to find their own way to the school event from California, which was right at the halfway point between Waterloo and San Fernando. They hired a taxi to take them to the nearest bus station and headed back to Port-of-Spain – When they arrived on the savannah in Port-of-Spain, they found the rest of their class and dispersed, trying to blend in to remain unseen. But Miss Take saw them and reported to Miss Conduct. Miss Take and Miss Conduct gathered the six near the back of the coach to await the headmaster's input.

The six had planned to evade all attempts at punishment should they be caught attending the school trip, and their plan included a surprise move! They had practiced it for weeks on end and were thrilled with the plan. O-Ryan would take the lead and Pepe, Claude, Freddie, Joe and Brian would follow.

As the headmaster approached them, O-Ryan shouted, "Shall we?" Immediately, the six jumped so high into the air that they almost touched the sky! With their arms and legs crossed, they appeared like six pairs of open scissors thrown up in the air - but only, they floated. They were up in the air for so long that everyone wondered whether the six would ever come back down.

Then suddenly, they heard O-Ryan shouting, his voice getting closer with each command. "Hey, guys, Land! Land! Land now!" And as they landed, O-Ryan tapped Pepe on the back, "Flying sure beats leap-frogging!"

The headmaster, caught by surprise, ordered that the six be brought to his camper van. Then he promptly organized for their parents to pick them up in the morning.
The six hurdled together for a seemingly long night. Freddie put on his MP3 player and streamed their favourite insect lullabies.

Author - Marie Laurencin

My big sister Cherrand, used to draw insects and animals on scrap paper and tell me stories of their lives when we were about five and seven years old. I was hooked. Soon, we began taking turns drawing and telling stories. The scrap paper came from the lithographic office where my great-grand-aunt, who raised us, used to clean. When the scrap paper was brought to us, bonded in thick book format, our joy was beyond what was ordinarily expressible by children! Those scrapbooks still hold the secrets of our magical story-making, drawing, and telling. I had no idea that after sojourning in the medical and pharmaceutical world, I would be returning to my roots both physically and metaphorically. I have returned to the Caribbean, and have once again turned my attention to writing about those creatures, telling tales of their tails, trails and trials.

Illustrator - Muriel Numao

Since I was small, I liked to draw. I liked it so much, that I filled all my books and even my school bench with pictures until my teachers told me to stop (which never lasted for long).

I spent many years studying for and working as as medical doctor until I remembered my passion and my dream: drawing and illustrating a children's book.

I very much enjoyed going through the story with the naughty frogs. I was the quiet type as a kid (and still am; quiet I mean, not a kid, although that's sometimes debatable) and so had a blast living it out on paper.

www.ingramcontent.com/pod-product-compliance
Lightning Source LLC
Chambersburg PA
CBHW080924190726
48293CB00010B/2674